The illustrations for this book were done in acrylic, ink, and pencil on plywood.
This book was edited by Megan Tingley and Julie Scheina and designed by Saho Fujii under the art direction of Patti Ann Harris.
The production was supervised by Charlotte Veaney, and the production editor was Christine Ma.
The text was set in Gararond Medium and the display type is Aram Caps. This book was printed on uncoated paper.

• Little, Brown and Company • Hachette Book Group • 237 Park Avenue • New York, NY 10017 • Visit our website at www.lb-kids.com • Little, Brown and Company is a division of Hachette Book Group, Inc. • The Little, Brown name and logo are trademarks of Hachette Book Group, Inc. • The publisher is not responsible for websites (or their content) that are not owned by the publisher. • First Edition: November 2013 • Library of Congress Cataloging-in-Publication Data • Stoop, Naoko, author, illustrator. • Red Knit Cap Girl to the Rescue / Naoko Stoop.—First edition. • pages cm • "Megan Tingley books." • Summary: "Red Knit Cap Girl and White Bunny, with help from Mr. Owl and the Moon, take to the high seas as they set off on a journey to help the lost Polar Bear Cub find his way back to his family and his arctic home"—Provided by publisher. • ISBN 978-0-316-22885-5 • [1. Polar bear—Fiction. 2. Bears—Fiction. 3. Lost children—Fiction. 4. Voyages and travels—Fiction.] 1. Title. • PZ7.S88353Rg 2012 • [E]—dc23 • 2012041465 • 10 9 8 7 6 5 4 3 2 1 • SC • Printed in China

RED KNIT CAP GIRL TO THE RESCUE

by NAOKO STOOP

Megan Tingley Books
LITTLE, BROWN AND COMPANY
New York   Boston

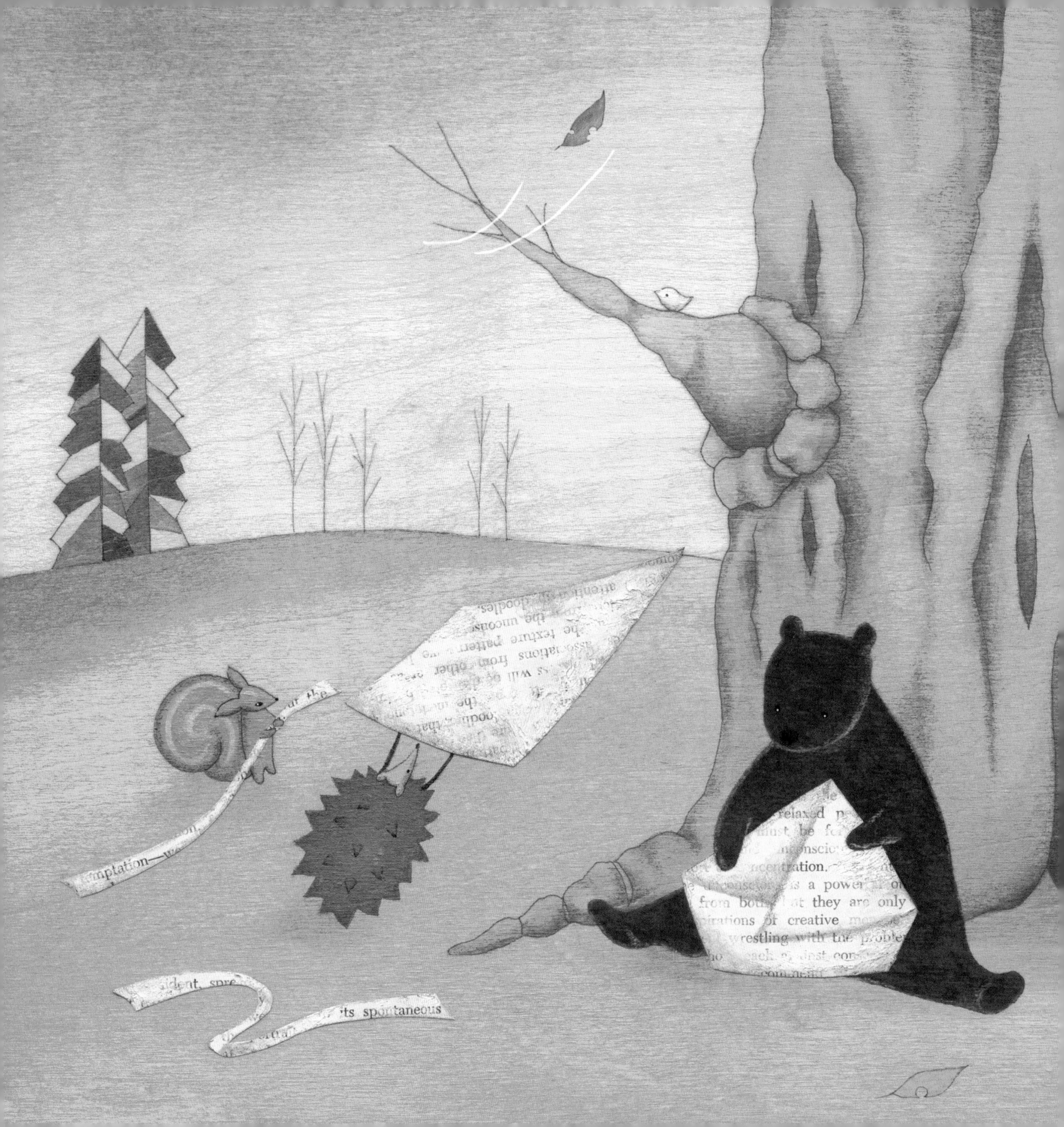

It is a windy day in the forest. Red Knit Cap Girl and her friends are playing together.

"What's that on the water?" asks Red Knit Cap Girl.
She looks through her telescope.

"IT'S A POLAR BEAR CUB!"

"He needs our help," she says.

"Come on, White Bunny!"

They bring Polar Bear Cub back to the forest. "Your family and friends must be looking for you," says Red Knit Cap Girl.

That evening, Red Knit Cap Girl calls out gently to the Moon.
"Moon, we are trying to find Polar Bear Cub's family.
Can you help us?"

Moon smiles and says, "Polar Bear Cub doesn't belong in our forest. You must take him to the North, where there is ice and snow and it is cold all year round."

The next day, Red Knit Cap Girl makes
a sturdy boat. Bear, Hedgehog, and Squirrel
help make the sail.

They sail north in search of Polar Bear Cub's home.
"I hope it's not too far away...." says Red Knit Cap Girl.
"Follow the light of the Moon," calls Owl.

They sail and sail until they encounter a storm. Dark clouds cover the sky.

Soon the clouds clear, and a friendly pair of Orcas
guide them back on course.

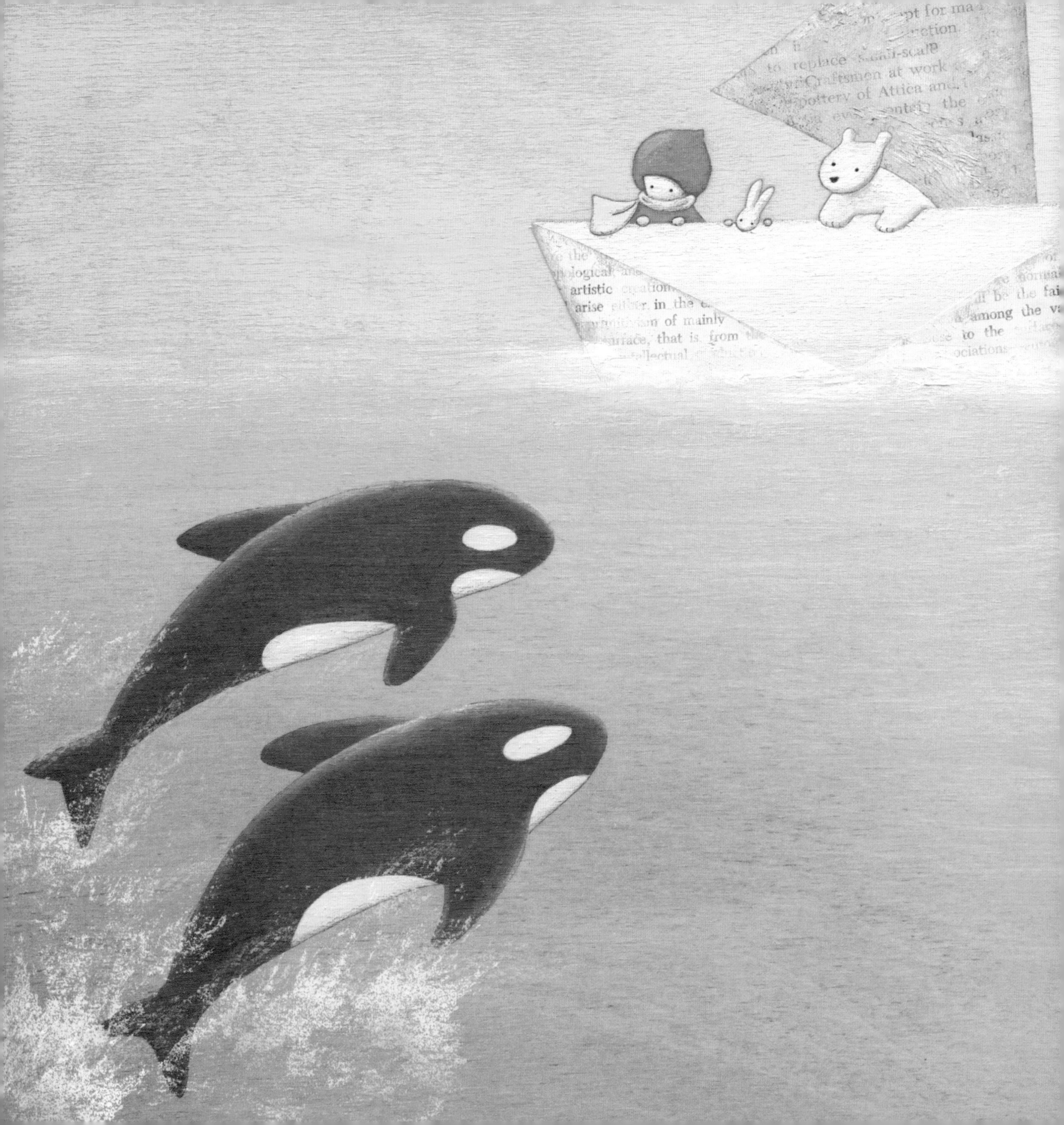

As they travel north, the air grows cool and the sky fills with color.
"How beautiful," says Red Knit Cap Girl.

She wonders if her forest friends are looking up at the same sky.

The next morning, they arrive at a land made of ice and snow!

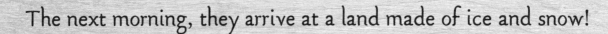

"Is this your home, Polar Bear Cub?" Red Knit Cap Girl asks.

Polar Bear Cub looks around.
There don't seem to be any other polar bears here.

Then they hear something coming toward them.

Mama!

Polar Bear Cub and Mama thank Red Knit Cap Girl
and White Bunny for bringing him home.

Soon, it is time for Red Knit Cap Girl and White Bunny
to return to the forest. "Good-bye, Polar Bear Cub!
We will always remember our journey together."

And they flew off into the starry sky.